THE
GATE

by

KEVIN JOHN WINDORF

QUINDORIAN PRESS

Cover photo and author photo by Jim Richards.
Cover photo and design by Kevin Windorf.

ISBN-10: 0692335889
ISBN-13: 978-0692335888 (Quindorian Press)

ALSO BY KEVIN JOHN WINDORF

The Serpent Bearer: 13 Stories of Suspense
Speaking In Tongues
Call From The Cabin
The Depth of My Drink, collected poems

www.kevinwindorf.com

for Olivia
that she may believe

.

For there is nothing either good or bad,
but thinking makes it so

— Shakespeare

PART ONE

T HE FULL MOON was not bright enough to reveal the acres of soybeans, but David knew by now that the field to the right of the road offered unending rows of the short plants. It was only his third trip to Jim's house, but he had learned to recognize the crop. The taller shadows on the left of the road were of course corn, the other staple of Virginia's Eastern Shore farmers. David could discern their rigid eye-high posture despite being a city dweller his whole life. There were square miles of stalks that would be solid and impenetrable or, if hewn smartly, a labyrinth of endless frustration.

"I don't want to go too fast on these roads —"

"I don't want you to," said Marianne.

"I'm just not too familiar with the sudden turns—"

"But you been here before, Daddy," said Emily from her car seat in the back of the Mercedes Benz.

"Yes, but I've never driven here at night."

"Was it always this dark?"

David smiled at the accidental poignancy of his four-year-old daughter's question.

"Daddy doesn't know, Em. Let him drive. You should be sleeping. Just close your eyes."

"I'll get scared, Mommy."

Under his breath, David said, "Yeah? Try driving on

these roads."

"Just take your time."

The two-lane country road had a single yellow line painted down its middle that served drivers well along the quarter mile straight stretches, but David suspected the line became irrelevant on the many curves that wound through the fields. The first two times to Jim's for a weekend of golf and fishing, David watched from the passenger seat as Jim would take the turns at speeds that made him nervous, or Jim would yield the road to passing locals who would race by even faster in their farm trucks, 4x4s and Jeeps.

David kept reminding himself that they were in no rush, and that it was far more important not to miss a turn. Without any semblance of street lighting – be it lampposts or traffic lights – drivers relied on headlights to illuminate the small green street signs with white reflective letters to identify roads. There were so few new drivers to the area though, that helping folks navigate the back roads between farms did not seem a concern of the county.

"How did Jim ever find this place?"

David peeked over at his wife. "You'd think he just got lost. Or lost a bet or something. But trust me, when you see his place in daylight, you'll understand why it's worth the five-hour drive."

Along a straightaway, they passed an old clapboard house, its dirty white shingles defined by the moonlight against the dark expanse behind it. Marianne thought that the small two-story home with the front porch looked quaint, until she noticed that the roof had collapsed on one side. She wondered how many years it had stood like that. Why would no one fix it?

"It's not much further. I'm pretty sure it's just two more rights, then we'll be on the road that leads into the gated community."

"What's a gated?" Emily wasn't asleep.

Marianne turned to her daughter. "It's where we're going on vacation."

David tried to be more enchanting. "It's like a castle, with a big strong gate all around."

"To make the princess safe?"

"That's right, Emmie." The proud father beamed.

"Safe from the monsters?"

David's smile fell. He dared a look at Marianne. "Nice going, Dad." She turned to Emily. "There are no monsters in Virginia, baby."

"DEER!" David shouted as he braked the Mercedes into a squealing stop. Emily screeched. Marianne was pulled towards the dashboard, then abruptly backwards as the seatbelt twisted her body.

"Jesus, David!"

"Christ, I almost hit it. It jumped out right in front of me."

"Where?!"

"There. It jumped off into the corn."

Marianne turned back to her crying daughter. "It's okay, Em, no one got hurt, it's just a deer."

"Monster…"

"No, just a deer. A big friendly deer, trying to scare the bejesus out of mommy and daddy."

Emily stopped crying then, but her eyes remained wide open in fear.

David slid his foot from the brake and onto the accelerator.

3

"Wait a minute." Marianne had her hand on his arm. "Give it a minute. There might be more. It's like they always travel in pairs."

"I think the sound of the brakes…"

Just then a second deer appeared on the right, walking out from the soybean field, slowly, almost majestically. It was a doe. She cocked her head and looked at the car.

"Monster!"

Emily's scream sent the doe bounding into the corn.

"Emily, please, it's just a deer. David, drive. Carefully." Marianne rubbed Emily's legs as they bounced in the car seat. "It's okay, Em, that was a mommy deer and I think she liked you. Did she give you a big smile? I think she winked at you."

Emily nodded her head in agreement. "Are we almost home in the gated?"

"Almost." David could feel the adrenaline still banging inside his chest. *Thank God I didn't hit that deer. What would we have done out here in the middle of nowhere? Christ I hope this wasn't a mistake.* "Here's the first right turn, just one more."

David kept his speed to the posted limit of 40, though he really wanted to drive slower and not risk any more wildlife encounters. This road offered the same two lanes, with soybeans on the right and corn on the left. Marianne kept one comforting hand on Emily's legs, as she maintained a watchful eye on the soybean fields, eager to see the next suicidal deer before it made a fateful leap.

David concentrated on the road, peering ahead for the final turn. Something caught his eye on the left, but when he risked a quick look, he could only see the forest-like corn. *What was that? Was the corn cut back in one sec-*

tion? Something dark was tucked in there. He tried to make sense of what his peripheral vision might have seen. He dared to take a peek in the rearview mirror.

His heart leaped as a section of corn suddenly lit up in a blaze of yellow light.

Instinctively his foot eased onto the brake.

"What it is, hon?" Marianne asked.

But the mystery was solved instantly as a pair of headlights emerged from the cornfield and turned onto the road behind the Mercedes. "Just a car," David said reassuringly.

"Well, watch where you're going."

"Yes, ma'am." David moved the car back up to 40, expecting the local driver to soon overtake and pass them. He went back to concentrating on looking for the upcoming intersection, but checking his rearview mirror every few seconds.

The headlights behind him shined high off the ground, so David knew that the vehicle was a pickup truck or an SUV. After a few minutes he grew curious that the driver hadn't sped up to pass. David took his foot off the gas and coasted a bit. Marianne didn't notice, as she sat intently looking out her side window. Emily seemed to have drifted back to sleep. The driver behind him maintained his distance. Why didn't he get closer?

"Are you slowing down?"

David turned to meet Marianne's question. "Um…" He looked back at the speedometer, as the needle just touched 30. "I thought I saw the turn." He pressed down on the accelerator. "My bad. You know, it all looks the same out here."

"We should have used the GPS."

"I told you, the development is off the grid. The roads are too new. The GPS wouldn't understand where we want to go."

"Do you?"

"Oh, good one. You enjoy the scenery and leave the driving to me."

"Scenery? I think it's called white moon over total darkness. There's nothing to see."

David pressed down and the car reached 45, 50 miles per hour.

"Aren't you worried about missing the turn?"

"Nah, I just remembered that there's a small white sign that says 'SeaView Turn Right' about 100 feet before the last turn."

David kept the car at 50 and watched in the rearview mirror as the driver behind him maintained the exact distance, about five car lengths. He was speeding up and slowing down just when David did. It was as if he didn't want to lose David. He didn't want to pass him, but he didn't want him to get away. That makes no sense.

First of all, maybe it's not a him. Maybe it's a woman. Maybe she's lost.

Down here? A woman in a truck, lost among the corn-fields? I don't think so.

Why was the truck in the cornfield to begin with? That wasn't a roadway. It was like a patch of dirt cut out in the corn. And the truck had its lights off. Like it was hiding.

David checked the mirror again. No change. The truck still shadowed him.

What if they were being followed? But why?

No, that's not the important question. The question is: what to do?

There were no options. No place to run and hide, no one to turn to.

The police? Use a cell phone to call the police and tell them a truck is driving safely five car lengths behind me and it "concerns" me? Even if I had to call the cops, I couldn't possibly tell them where we are. The cell phone might not even work here.

The police. Of course. It's probably a cop car. An SUV. He was hiding in the corn as a speed trap. Brilliant.

But I wasn't speeding. And that's why he hasn't pulled me over. He was probably curious about the out of state plates. Followed me to check us out. Clean record. We're good. The cop could be driving back to the precinct house or whatever they call it down here. Or maybe he's just driving home.

"There's the sign." Marianne was excited to finally see something in the darkness.

"What?"

"The sign, David, the sign. There. 'SeaView Turn Right.'"

David slowed the car. Up ahead the road ended, meeting another country road running perpendicular. Dead ahead, on the other side of the road, was yet another wall of corn behind a yellow sign with a black, two-headed horizontal arrow offering the choice of left or right.

David checked the mirror: the truck had also slowed down. At the end of the road stood a slightly tilted stop sign whose red octagon was weather-beaten and scarred, pocked by pellets it seemed. A few feet past the sign, David brought the Mercedes to a complete stop. He checked the road in both directions. Darkness.

Then he peeked up at the mirror and paused. The truck

had also stopped, some five car lengths back.

Suddenly David spun the wheel to the left and sped onto the new road, loose gravel kicking up under the car's tires.

"What are you doing? It's a right turn!"

"I know."

"The sign said 'right.' You said so yourself."

"I know, I just want to see something."

David drove about fifty yards then stopped. He looked hard into the darkness reflected in the rearview mirror.

"David?"

"That truck behind us. I think it was following us. I didn't want him to see we were going to SeaView."

"Following us?" Marianne laughed. "Are you kidding me? What are you a spy? Give me a break."

"I'm just saying."

"Saying what: We're in the middle of nowhere and suddenly a 'bad man' is following you?"

David felt annoyed, and maybe a little embarrassed, but Marianne naming his fear out loud deepened his sense of discomfort.

"Where's the bad man, Mommy?" Emily stirred.

David shot Marianne a look, redirecting her criticism.

She leaned back and rubbed her daughter's legs. David peered into the rearview mirror but could see only the back of Marianne's head. He quickly leaned to the left to check the side view mirror. The angle wasn't exactly right. He adjusted it with a button on the door, to see more of the road behind him. But all he could see was the red of his brake light illuminating a small patch of the darkness.

He watched anxiously as Marianne cooed Emily back to sleep again. As she sat back, she whispered, "Can we go now?" It wasn't a question.

David drove another twenty feet, slowly, as if to confirm that it was his decision, then made a precise K-turn on the narrow two-lane road. He was very conscious of the three-foot deep ditches on either side of the road, knowing that a slip down one would maroon them for the night. With each angle of the car's turn, the headlights flooded the rows and rows of impenetrable cornstalks with an eerie white light that made their rigid stillness seem skeletal.

David edged the car along the small shoulder, turning it back to face the road towards SeaView. He looked at Marianne for a moment but said nothing. Her eyes were closed. Was she suppressing anger? Fatigue? Or did she feel it, too?

David accelerated and the car shot into the dark, its high beams blazing the trail before them like a torch flaring into a cave. As the car crossed the intersection where he had turned, David looked quickly to his right, expecting to see the truck, or at least its headlights. But nothing. He drove on.

Where had the truck gone? It obviously didn't follow him with the left turn, and he didn't see it turn right towards SeaView, he had specifically watched for that. In this darkness, headlights and brake lights would clearly give away any movement. Unless they were turned off, and the truck had parked. With the driver just waiting.

David accelerated. The cornfields eventually conceded to woods. The trees were tall and thick, arching from both sides over the road. The night sky and the moon were blocked out. It was a different kind of darkness now.

"How much further?"

"Less than two minutes," David said evenly.

Something darted onto the road, then back just as quickly into the woods.

"What was that?!"

David smiled, "*That* was a fox."

"A fox? No way." Marianne's voice betrayed her disbelief as disappointment in missing the opportunity to see a fox in the wild.

"Sure. Someone's got to eat the deer. Keep the population down." David kidded with her because he felt oddly triumphant that the appearance of the fox confirmed his suspicions about the night.

"Fox don't eat deer."

"Okay. But ducks, and geese. Field mice. Bunnies."

"Dad, remember the back seat."

David reached up and tilted the rearview mirror an inch so he could see whether Emily was still asleep in the car seat. She was sleeping soundly, her head completely tipped to one side. Dreaming of bunnies, hopefully, in a land of no foxes.

David reset the mirror. When he checked the angle, he felt his heart tighten. In the mirror, he saw two small white dots in the darkness. Moving. Closer.

Headlights.

David accelerated. The car was now doing 50. Trees flashed past the window like a strobe light.

"Quick, open the glove compartment. Top sheet of paper. Directions from Jim. Top right corner, the six hand-written numbers. I need those. Quick."

Marianne had jumped right away, no questions.

Up ahead something was in the road. The headlights clarified the image as the car raced towards it. It was a gate.

A black wrought iron gate, some twelve feet high, twenty

feet across, spanned the road, secured at either side by a wide red brick pillar, topped by an ornately carved pine-apple of white painted cement.

The name "SeaView" was emblazoned on a brass plaque on the left pillar. A matching plaque on the right stated, "Private Property."

"We're there." Marianne was excited, relieved.

"Not yet."

"What's wrong?"

David braked the car to a full stop, lining up his door perfectly aside a lone metal pole that stood four feet high on the side of the road. At the top of the black pole was a simple keypad, with numbers zero to nine arrayed like buttons on a telephone.

David pushed the control on his door and the driver's side window whirred down.

"The numbers."

Marianne responded, a little pissed off at David's tone. "Seven, seven, six. Four, three, two."

As she spoke, David punched the numbers on the keypad. As soon as he hit the number two, the gate unlocked with a loud decisive metallic noise, and it began to move. The iron gate, whose bars were only six inches apart, split in half in the middle of the road and each side rolled away in a sweeping arc. A set of large steel wheels rolled across the smooth macadam roadway, pulled by the hydraulic motor that operated the gate.

The process was steady and deliberate for safety, but its slowness gripped David and tightened the vice in his chest. He didn't wait for the arc to be completed. Once the opening was big enough for the Mercedes, David floored it and the car shot through the gap in the gate.

"David!"

He snapped back: "It's all right." Twenty feet past the gate, he slammed on the brakes. The tires squealed.

"What the hell are you doing?!"

David watched the rearview mirror. "Come on, come on."

The gate completed its precision operation and was now fully opened. It waited a calculated measure of five seconds for safety, then, sensing no vehicle outside the entrance or between its infrared sensors, the gate began to close. "Come on, come on." David put his fist to his lips.

Marianne was startled by David's intensity. She turned and looked out the rear window, above Emily's head. Past the closing arms of the gate, she could see approaching headlights. "What is that?"

David sat motionless, as if hiding. But he felt completely exposed. The field mouse frozen in fear, hoping the circling hawk has lost it against the ground brush.

"David…?"

"It's that truck."

"What truck?"

"The one that was following us."

"You're crazy. There wasn't a truck following us. You saw that yourself."

"It's coming now."

"Then what are you waiting for?"

"You'll see."

Marianne stared out the rear window, unconsciously resting her face on the headrest. She watched as the headlights became slightly larger, each halo tighter, as the vehicle approached. The two sides of the gate continued their slow path towards each other. The wrought iron bars made the headlights blink at Marianne as they moved across her vision.

"Hold on." David suddenly threw the gearshift into reverse and sped backwards, then just as quickly slammed on the brakes.

Marianne twisted again in her seat. "Stop it!"

The gate clanged shut, the electronic mechanism beeping to confirm the gate was now locked.

"Jesus, David!"

"It's okay."

"What are you doing?!"

David watched the mirror. The headlights had stopped moving. Waiting in the darkness beyond, at what David estimated to be forty feet, a shadowy outline hinted at a pickup truck.

"There is a truck!" Marianne was surprised that her voice broke.

"Don't worry. The gate can't open while we're on the sensors."

"What? Why should I be worried?"

"That truck was hiding in the corn, then started to follow us, then it went into hiding again, and now he's back. Waiting for us to make a move."

"Who's hiding, Mommy?" Emily pushed her fists into her eyes as she tried to wake up.

"David, do you hear yourself? This is paranoia beyond belief. Did you ever think that maybe the guy just lives here? And you're blocking his path."

"Yeah? Why doesn't he honk?"

"Who's honking, Mommy?"

"Oh Emily, no one's honking, why don't you go back to sleep and you'll wake up in a nice cozy bed. Okay?"

David reached up and adjusted the mirror. He wanted the driver in the truck to know he was watching. "I learned from Jim that the gate won't open, or close, if the sensors know there's something within ten feet of the gate. That's how it knows when to close." David's words re-assured him, but Marianne felt bewildered by her husband.

"Are we just going to sit here?"

David didn't answer.

A low rumbling sound. Thunder? No. Was the truck revving its engine?

The rumbling stopped.

Ten seconds passed. Emily was asleep again. The truck hadn't moved.

Suddenly, a faint sound hit the windshield. Both David and Marianne looked for the source. Was it just a bug?

Then another pop, followed quickly by more. "Rain." David looked back into the mirror.

"Great. Are we going to just sit here, in the rain? Look at that." Marianne pointed out the front windshield. Rain was falling fiercely further up the road. The Mercedes' headlights cut two precise spotlights into the darkness ahead and revealed a downpour of rain rapidly moving along the road towards the car. Thunder boomed in the distance. The rain was suddenly upon the Mercedes, beating a violent cacophony on the hood and roof.

"Jesus, it's going to wake Emily," Marianne said.

David tried to watch as the wall of rain overtook the gate, then the truck, but the visibility was blurred as the cascade of rain slid down the back window. He quickly grabbed the door handle, opened the door and leapt up to stand next to the car.

"David!"

He shielded his eyes with his hand. Within seconds his shirt was soaked, his hair matted. But he saw what he needed to see.

The truck began to slowly pull away, reversing as the rain beat down on it. The headlights becoming smaller, duller in the rain. After about twenty yards, the light slid sideways and shone briefly into the trees on the right of the road. On the opposite side, a momentary flare of red, and David knew the truck was reversing in a K-turn. Then two red lights moved down the road and into the darkness, beyond the rain, until David could see them no more.

David slipped back into the Mercedes and shut the door.

"Well?"

David looked at his wife. "It's gone."

"So?"

"So, I guess he didn't live here after all."

"Fine. Can we go?"

"Yes. But as soon as we get to Jim's house, I'm calling the police."

"As soon as we get to the house, I'm putting Emily to bed," Marianne said. "Why don't you just call Jim?"

"What's he going to do, back in New York?"

"Well, the police aren't going to do anything. Nothing happened."

David looked away from Marianne and turned on the windshield wipers. "Hold on." He drove as fast as he thought safe. Thick raindrops pounced high on the roadway, set ablaze by the Mercedes' headlights. In the distance, a small solitary light became a yellow beacon of hope for David. It was a porch light at Jim's house, which stood otherwise invisible at the end of the road, overlooking the ocean-bound inlet beyond.

In the darkness outside of the gate, the twin white headlights of the truck came to life. The truck edged into the dim circle of light shining down from the lamppost, a hapless, silent sentinel. The driver reached up and pressed a plastic remote control clipped to the sun visor.

As the rain continued to beat down, the locking mechanism automatically disengaged and the gate began to come apart, splitting open into two moving fences, mirrored in design, arcing away from each other, into the darkness beyond.

PART TWO

RAINWATER SHOT UP from the road as the Mercedes raced along the wet pavement. The wipers pushed the torrent of splattering raindrops from the windshield. David's eyes were wide, glancing from mirror to mirror, side to side. He knew there could be deer. There could be all kinds of nighttime critters dashing out of the darkness. But he remembered that the road was smooth and at the end of it stood Jim's house.

The rain clouds obscured the full moon and any hint of a house in the distance, save for the dot of yellow that David knew to be the porch light.

He wouldn't risk looking at Marianne, but he could sense her anxiety.

Part of him hoped he had been wrong – it might be safer to risk his wife's wrath than what his fear could only imagine.

Marianne leaned forward a little in the passenger's seat, peering into the side view mirror, looking for the truck. Looking for anything. But there was nothing to see. The angle was wrong, the rain was too dense, it was too damn dark. Or maybe there was just nothing to see. The pit in her stomach belied her anger, but she wondered if it was just fear. What if David had been right? Who was in that pickup truck?

Once they left the highway that bisected the Eastern Shore of Virginia, dividing the bay side from the ocean side, all the roads, including those in the SeaView gated community, fell off on either side into three-foot ditches. The rain did not puddle on the asphalt and the downpour would just stream away. Still David wouldn't risk doing more than 40 over the half-mile stretch. With four-year-old Emily in the back seat, there just seemed to be too much at stake.

"There it is." He announced. Not relief but determination in his voice.

"What? Where?"

"Eleven o'clock. That yellow light. That's Jim's house. Thank God."

Marianne tried to break the tension, "Don't you think you're being a little dramatic?"

"The light is on. That means the power is on. I was afraid the storm would knock out the power."

"Does that happen a lot?"

"You kidding? His house is right on the inlet that leads to the ocean. Jim has told me about some major storms here. Ferocious. Always knocking out the power. But he says the lightning is fantastic." He added, as if to himself, "I always wanted to see that."

Marianne heard him and said, "Careful what you wish for."

David peered at the rearview mirror. Again, he questioned whether he'd made the right decision to bring his wife and daughter to the middle of nowhere in the middle of the night, just to avoid the daytime traffic that might have stolen a few precious hours from his birthday weekend get-away. Nothing's worth this feeling.

A quick flash of lightning brightened the night sky over the ocean, and Marianne could see a full silhouette of the house. Despite the rain, she could now make out the outline of Jim's house. She saw that the two-story structure had a gabled roof with a chimney running up the right end of the house. It was much larger than David had led her to believe. But the size didn't seem to give her comfort. "Looks big. Hope we don't get lost in it."

They were close enough now for David to see the two brick pillars that stood on either side of the driveway that opened onto Jim's property and ended at an attached garage. Although there had been several cross-streets leading to the half dozen other houses in SeaView, the main road ended right at Jim's house. Because of that, Jim had created a bookend feel to the road by replicating the brick pillars from the front gate, including the concrete pineapples that adorned the tops. When Jim had explained the design concept to David and that pineapples were a symbol of hospitality, David kidded his friend that the bricks were "as welcoming as a cemetery."

The brick motif was continued along the base of Jim's house from the foundation up three feet to where yellow shingles then completed the exterior of the house. David remembered Jim explaining how the inlet surged during one hurricane all the way up to the house but not higher than the bricks, so the house was saved from any flooding.

The rain continued to pelt the Mercedes as David finally slowed down. He eased the car between the driveway pillars and quickly parked close to the walkway that led to the front door of the house.

"What about the garage?" asked Marianne.

"I don't think there's room for our car," David said

quickly. His only thought was to get his family into that house and to get on the phone.

Marianne said, "I'll deal with Emily. Go in and get some lights on."

"Right." David grabbed the set of keys that Jim had given him from the pocket on the driver's door. He raced out into the rain and bounded across the pavement and up the front steps. He stood under the yellow porch light and fumbled with the six keys on the key ring, which also held a rabbit's foot, dyed red. The rain further soaked the shoulders of David's shirt, and drops slid from his matted hair into his eyes. Key after key failed to open the door.

Marianne barked, "What's wrong!?" as she shuffled up behind him carrying Emily and her overnight bag.

"Mommy, it's raining."

"I know, Emmie. It's fun, isn't it?"

The last key worked. "Finally," David grunted as he pushed the door open.

Emily said, "I'm getting wet."

"Me, too," Marianne cooed, "but now we're going inside the nice big house."

David knew to reach to the right of the open door to find the light switches. With one swipe he hit three switches and the house came alive with bright white light.

"Ow, Mommy."

"It's okay, Emmie, Daddy just turned on the lights so we can see where we're going." Marianne looked at her husband, not sure about his stress. "I need to get her into dry pajamas and into bed. Where?"

"Top of the stairs. Two bedrooms. Put her in the one with the double bed. Less likely she'll fall out and get hurt."

"Fine. We can get the rest of the bags tomorrow."

Marianne headed up the steps to the second floor, with Emily snug on her hip, her bag swinging from her shoulder. David slipped off his wet shoes and went to the kitchen looking for the house phone. But first he grabbed a dishtowel to mop off his face. As he buried his eyes in the towel, he laughed at himself: he had taken off his shoes instinctively. Jim kept his house "shoe-free" – one of his obsessions, David thought, but one he agreed with. Between dirt and pesticides and other detritus that you traipsed through all day, why bring that danger into your house?

"Shit." David spoke out loud as he turned slowly to look at the front door. He realized that he had left it open. Had he actually thought Marianne would be able to close it with Emily in her arms?

The door stood about two feet open. Outside the porch light illuminated the heavy raindrops that splashed down onto the front steps. The light bulb seemed to sizzle. There was one small moth flitting between drops, desperate to touch the bulb.

David dropped the dishtowel to the floor. He felt frozen, his legs locked by the weight of fear. He sensed some-thing was about to happen. Would the door suddenly swing shut? Or would someone barge in and...?

"David!" Marianne called down from upstairs in an exaggerated whisper. "David."

He recovered at the sound of his wife's voice and immediately headed towards the staircase by the front door. "What?" he said, mimicking her whisper.

"There's no hot water."

Without even thinking about it, David reached out and

closed the front door. Looking down at the doorknob, he realized what he'd done, then quickly turned the lock on the handle and flipped the dead bolt into place. He leaned on the door and peered out the small window at eye level. But he couldn't see anything past the yellow glare of the porch light, where the solitary moth still danced despite the rain.

"David. Hot water."

"What? Just let it run."

Feeling distracted David headed back to the kitchen, picking up the dishtowel and thinking: phone. "Damn," he spoke out loud. He paced back to the staircase and whispered, "Marianne."

"No reason to whisper, she's awake."

"I forgot. I need to turn on the hot water heater."

"Why?"

"Jim keeps it off when he's not here. He left me instructions. Somewhere." David looked around the hallway. "Let me just call the police, then I'll deal with the hot water."

David felt frustrated. His fear – no, "concern" – had been derailed by the routine of life. Turning into the kitchen and seeing the phone silent in its cradle, he felt foolish having said the word "police."

He reached for the phone, but instead, placed his hand on the cool gray granite countertop. He leaned his weight forward, relaxing his body and directing his tension down his arm, through his spread fingers and on to the coolness of the granite. He closed his eyes and thought about the stand-off with the pickup truck at the gate in the rain. He quickly remembered the threat he felt, the vulnerability... but was it just imagined?

Then he pictured the pickup truck lying in wait, hidden in the corn, and how it had stalked him. Was "stalked" the right word? No. David felt toyed with. A cat. With a mouse.

David opened his eyes, aware that he was clenching his jaw fiercely. His anger was palpable.

He grabbed the phone and headed into the living room. He stood before the bay window that looked out onto the front yard and the road that trailed back to the gate that kept the world out of SeaView. He could see nothing in the darkness, save the reflection of the lights in the kitchen behind him. He recognized that the movement in the window was his own reflection moving the phone to his ear.

But there was no sound.

Looking at the phone keypad, David pushed the power button off, then on again. The green light promised him that the phone was charged, but still, there was no dial tone.

He stared out into the darkness again. Was the phone service down because of the storm? Or because…? No, the electricity in the house was still on. The storm was just messing with the reception. He slid his cellphone from his pants pocket. As expected, the home screen showed no reception bars. From his prior trips to SeaView, David knew that cellphones couldn't pick up a signal due to the remoteness of the gated community. But the house phone had always been reliable.

Of course, he'd never been at the house during a storm. But Jim had bragged about the ferocity of the storms that would barrel across the Eastern Shore. David had been warned.

Although there were a dozen exceptionally tall pine trees on Jim's property, for the most part, SeaView was open to the inlet and the breezes from the Atlantic Ocean about two miles away. With nothing to slow it down, the wind could become deadly, pushing the waves before it and leaving uprooted pines behind it.

There was a startling flash of lightning. For a moment the front yard flared with white light and David's reflection in the bay window was gone. Just as quickly the outside world was sucked back to darkness and the only light came from over David's shoulders in the kitchen.

As expected, a clap of thunder followed. It was so intense that it seemed to shake the house. David could hear Emily scream upstairs in the bathroom, followed by Marianne's comforting words.

But David wasn't distracted. In his mind's eye, he played back the image the lightning had revealed, freezing it for detection. He saw the outline of the Mercedes off to the right. He saw the two brick pillars, with their pineapple ornaments, standing about 15 feet apart. He saw the road, empty. The wet grassy field on the other side of the road that led to a large pond, empty.

It was then that he remembered the motion detectors. From the far-left corner of the house and the far-right corner of the garage, two outdoor lights with motion detectors were directed to cover half the driveway and the entire front of the house. On his last visit, David had held the ladder as Jim adjusted the light over the garage, which had been loosened by a storm. Jim explained that the detectors caught all kinds of nocturnal visitors to his house, from possums and woodchucks to rabbits and deer. Plenty of deer, Jim said. In fact, he told David that the motion detectors once threw their light onto a pair of deer mating. "They didn't seem too embarrassed," Jim had said.

He told David that the coolest thing he'd seen was a family of foxes – a vixen and three kits. Jim had asked David to help him figure out how to set up a camera to be triggered by the motion detectors to capture the unsuspecting creatures. But they never got around to that project. It was just one of their many ideas, shared over cigars and scotches on the back deck of the house, after a relaxing round of golf. Relaxing. That was the word. Vacation. Relaxation. He looked at the phone in his hand and felt foolish.

David consciously took a deep breath. This was a vacation home. One of the most beautiful, tranquil places he'd ever been to. It was time to think of it like that.

If that truck was in fact following them on the road to SeaView, it couldn't get through the gate. If it did get through the gate, it couldn't get on the property without the motion detectors warning them. Besides, David knew where Jim kept a .22 rifle (for target practice off the back deck). David smiled at himself. "Right." He knew he'd never need to resort to that.

Deep breath. No one could get into SeaView. No one could get onto the property undetected. No one could get into the house.

But something ate at David. He wasn't sure what kept him from relaxing. Maybe it's the rain, he thought. Maybe it's worrying about Marianne and Emily. No, something wasn't right.

David turned from the bay window and walked through the kitchen into the small sunroom that sat off the back deck. The only other way into the house, besides the front door, he remembered, was the back-deck door. He placed his hand on the knob, confirmed it was locked, but rattled the door for good measure. He could feel the bolt was thrown.

Looking beyond the back deck, where a solitary light shone in the rain at the end of a small pier, David thought about Jim's house, picturing it from the outside. It was a long house, its wide front facing the road that led from the SeaView entrance gate. The two-car garage was on the far left, then the front door with its yellow porch light, then the living room's bay window. Moving to the right there was the hallway with framed bare windows that provided an unobstructed view of SeaView's pond. Driving through the rain, David hadn't pointed it out to Marianne. It was too late tonight, but on an earlier visit, David appreciated the beauty of the setting sun as it threw an orange reflection across the pond before it disappeared into the shadowy pines lining the western perimeter of SeaView.

At the end of the hall, a staircase led to a second-floor bedroom that Jim used as his office and television room. Under that room, a left turn from the hallway led to the master bedroom and bathroom. The bedroom was adjacent to the sunroom in the back of the house, but there was no connecting door.

Standing in the sunroom, David was confident that there were only two entrances to the house. He had locked the front door himself, and now he knew that the back door was locked too.

He had to relax.

Outside the sunroom, the back deck, made of concrete and brick, stood three feet above a hearty grass lawn that sloped down to the marshy edge of the inlet. About fifty feet from the house, a narrow pier rose above the marsh and another fifty feet later ended at a small dock where Jim's boat was tied up, lit by a single white light. The steadfastness of that light, despite the rain that continued to teem, lifted David. He thought about the boat and two great trips he had had with Jim, catching flounder early in the morning. They hadn't gone far in the boat before finding a few good spots where the inlet opened up and the bottom dropped down to about twenty-five feet. They never did take the boat out to the Atlantic for more challenging fishing. Jim told David that if they let the boat float with the current, either they would get stuck in the marsh reeds that lined the banks or they'd eventually make it all the way out to the ocean.

Their fishing excursions were usually very quick, as they liked to get in a full day of golf before coming home to a dinner of flounder that Jim would filet and fry himself.

The thought of fishing reminded David that he promised Marianne to take her and Emily out in the boat. Marianne was more comfortable around boats than he was, but he just wasn't crazy about bringing a four-year-old onto a boat for the first time. Too many things were unpredictable. One time, David and Jim were standing on the dock enjoying cigars when they spotted the dorsal fin of a shark, albeit a small one, about three feet in length. Jim said it was probably a young sandbar shark. It swam right past the dock, further up the inlet. They watched as it went about another twenty yards, suddenly splashed about, then turned and headed back down the inlet towards the ocean. "Got something," Jim said. "Like what?" David asked. "Something small. Maybe a croaker, maybe a crab." David blew out a trail of cigar smoke,

"Remind me not to cool off my feet sitting on the edge of the dock." "Hey, maybe fewer toes would improve your golf game."

David had not mentioned the shark story to Marianne, but he'd be sure to do so before they got in the boat in the morning. He wondered how Marianne was managing with Emily upstairs.

He moved quietly to the foot of the staircase by the front door. He whispered, "Mar'e?" No answer. At the top of the stairs, Marianne had plugged in a nightlight they'd brought from home. On the second floor, the short hallway offered doors to a bathroom and two bedrooms. "Mar'e?"

Suddenly, Marianne appeared. "Shhh. She's asleep. Again."

"Good. Need anything?"

"What's the story with the hot water?"

"Shit. I forgot."

"How could you forget? It was the only thing you needed to do."

David hesitated. He wanted to defend himself, he wanted to explain how he'd gotten himself convinced that they were safe. He wanted to show his courage in not needing to call the police – even though he simply couldn't because of the phone reception being out. But he didn't want a prolonged conversation in whispered voices.

"I'll go do it now. The heater is in a closet off the master bedroom."

"What? Why isn't in the basement?"

"There's no basement."

"Oh." David turned to go but Marianne whispered again, "David. We'll sleep up here, in the other room."

"In the twin beds?"

"I don't want to leave Emily up here by herself."

At the sound of her name, Emily woke up. "Mommy? Mommy, who are you talking to?"

"Just Daddy." Marianne made a gesture of exasperation at David.

He whispered up to her, "You know, the three of us can all sleep in the master bedroom. It's got a king size bed."

"Sounds ideal. Just go get me some hot water."

Marianne headed back to the bedroom where Emily sat, propped up on pillows, hugging her blanket and three stuffed animals, all rabbits. "I don't want to take a bath."

"Don't worry, the hot water's not for a bath. It's just for…" Marianne searched for a word, not sure how a four-year-old would understand the desire for running hot and cold water in a house. "It's for living in this house."

"We live here now?"

"No, just this weekend. For vacation. Now you go to sleep and we'll start vacation tomorrow morning. The sun will be out, and it will be bright and shining and we'll go for a boat ride and we might see all kinds of fun fish and birds and maybe even a deer."

Emily looked at her mother, unsure. "Monster?"

"Of course not, there are no monsters on vacation."

Marianne scooched Emily under the covers, pulling her blanket under her chin and squeezing the three plush rabbits close to her daughter's cheeks. She bent low to kiss her on the forehead and whispered, "Good night, princess, Mommy and Daddy will be right next door."

Marianne left the door open so Emily could see the nightlight in the hall. She ducked into the bathroom where she had dropped her overnight bag when she had Emily use the toilet and brush her teeth. Marianne set up her toiletries along the sink, then she found David's toothbrush and razor in the bag. Turning on the tap, she felt the water. It was still icy cold. "Come on house, make it hot already."

Marianne peeked down the hall at Emily. Convinced her daughter was already asleep again, she headed downstairs and straight into the kitchen.

She quickly assessed the appliances, which all seemed new and rarely used, and the décor. She liked the tile on the backsplash and along the counter with its blue and white motif of seashells. But she didn't care for the matching ceramic dolphins that adorned the wall on either side of the window above the sink.

Doesn't really matter, she thought, not my kitchen. What would you expect from a bachelor? Marianne spoke out loud, "I'm starving." She opened the refrigerator and was not surprised to see a few jars of condiments and a good supply of bottles of beer. There was no food to speak of – why should there be? Jim wasn't expected to stock the house with groceries for them. It was nice enough that he loaned his house to David for the weekend getaway.

Marianne thought that part of the reason for the invitation to use his house was to reassure her that Jim in fact existed. He and David met about four years earlier at some sales convention. Marianne had never met Jim – never even seen a photo of him. She'd tease David that Jim didn't exist and that his supposed trips to Virginia to fish and to play golf were just ruses to cover up a torrid affair that David was having with a mysterious woman.

Looking around the kitchen, Marianne realized something else was missing from the house. Photographs. No framed pictures anywhere. Again she stopped herself: would a bachelor actually have a magnet photo of himself on the refrigerator? She realized she'd not been to the master bedroom, so maybe… but, she thought to herself, a bachelor with a photo of himself in his bedroom would be a little creepy.

Still, don't fishermen always have photos of themselves, standing proudly on a boat or on a dock, holding some oversized fish all dead-eyed and slimy?

And what about golf? Shouldn't there be a prerequisite foursome photo from a charity outing?

Marianne leaned against the kitchen sink and looked again at the room. All neat and tidy. Stainless steel teapot, a set of carving and steak knives poised in a wooden block, a row of four matching coffee mugs behind the glass door of one cabinet. She opened a few rollup cabinet doors and discovered a microwave, a blender, and several bottles of booze. Scotch, bourbon, rum, others she didn't recognize. She wondered why no vodka, but then thought to check the freezer. There she found a tall bottle, half full, of an imported brand. But then she spied a frozen pizza.

"Oh yes. Come to mama," she said aloud.

She knew she could replace Jim's bachelor stash tomorrow, so she didn't hesitate to tear open the box and slide the pizza into the microwave. A quick review of the various buttons and soon the microwave was whirring and rotating the dish. Marianne closed her eyes and smiled at the thought of beginning her vacation by pilfering a frozen pizza.

Down the hall, David successfully retrieved the all-important closet key from the hiding spot Jim had described, a wooden duck decoy on his dresser. The duck's head was on a hinge, virtually invisible. David had tipped the head back to reveal the silver key. He had to remember to return it to the duck otherwise he'd be in big trouble with Jim. Although David had never gone into this bedroom closet, his friend explained that it was where he'd find the hot water heater – kept off during the weeks Jim wasn't in the house – and, more importantly, it was where Jim stored his .22 rifle for safety. Jim and David had used the gun for target practice off the back deck, shooting at empty plastic bottles placed atop the pilings of the pier. The men allowed themselves just a few minutes with the rifle before their pre-dinner cocktails, which Jim never served until the rifle was safely stored in its case and returned to the closet. David especially enjoyed the target shooting because he was quite good at it. He'd never fired any type of gun before – his proficiency seemed to come naturally.

David turned the key in the lock and opened the closet. He flicked on the wall switch and was surprised how large the closet was. David spotted the wooden rifle case leaning in the far corner. Instinctively he went to it to confirm that it was locked, but first he made sure the door was closed behind him. He didn't want Marianne to suddenly pop in and get curious. She would have no tolerance for sleeping in a house with a gun, let alone finding out that her husband had been playing Wild Bill when she thought he was only playing golf.

David was relieved that the case was locked. He grabbed the top with his hand and gave it a shake. By the weight, he knew the rifle was in there. Reassured, he turned his attention to the hot water heater.

He wasn't surprised to see a note taped to the wall, with handwritten instructions and a schematic drawing indicating which switches to turn. Jim was very precise and careful with his possessions. He was happy to lend out his house, but he wanted everything done correctly.

David followed the instructions and smiled when he heard the system kick on. "Hot water, here we come." Satisfied with himself, David hit the light switch with his right hand and turned the doorknob with his left. But the knob didn't turn. He immediately flicked the light back on. There was no button on the handle to lock the door – because there's no reason to lock a closet from the inside – so David tried the knob again. But it wouldn't turn. It was locked from the outside. "Oh, that's brilliant." David released a heavy sigh. He imagined the mockery from Marianne for locking himself in the closet.

But then he pictured the key in the lock. He couldn't have locked himself in. The key had to be turned inside the lock. He realized that Marianne must already be on the other side of the door, ready to mock him.

"Very funny, Mar'e. You know, you're the one who wanted the hot water. I can just as easily turn it off again. Now open the door, okay? You had your laugh."

But there was no answer.

Down the hall Marianne was still waiting in the kitchen for the pizza to heat up, so she continued to snoop around. Standing next to the dinner table just off the kitchen, she looked out the back window. In the distance, a small light shone at the end of a pier. She assumed it must be where Jim's motorboat was moored. But otherwise she couldn't see anything in the darkness beyond the deck that was lit up by the back-deck lights. Then she saw a movement that gave her a momentary start until she realized it was her own reflection. In fact she could see the reflection of the window behind her, but nothing in the darkness that shrouded the front of the house.

Curious, she went over to the front door to see if there were more lights for outside. Looking at the light switches – there was a bank of some four switches – she noticed that all but one were in the on position. She moved to the last switch, wondering if David left that one off on purpose or that he just hadn't reached it. She wanted to see what else would light up.

Just as Marianne touched the switch, she felt a sudden draft on her ankles. She turned and flinched as the microwave beeped loudly. "Christ." Realizing it was only the pizza, she hit the last light switch – turning on the pair of outdoor lights equipped with motion detectors that David had inadvertently missed.

Looking out the window, at the driveway now bathed in yellow light, Marianne screamed at the top of her lungs.

Parked in front of the house, at the end of the driveway, between the two brick pillars, was the pickup truck.

PART THREE

D AVID WAS STUNNED to hear Marianne scream. His annoyance at being locked in the closet had been growing towards anger, but when he heard his wife scream, all emotion turned to dread. Nothing would make her scream like that other than physical pain. Had she fallen?

"Marianne! Marianne! What happened?"

As he jiggled the doorknob, leaning on the door with his shoulder, hoping to pry it open just by sheer will, David thought he could here Emily wailing. But the rain continued to pelt the house, making Emily's cries seem fragile and distant.

Was Emily hurt too?

"God damn it! Let me out." David screamed at the door itself, as he banged his fists on it, then slammed his shoulder against it.

Marianne's body quaked with the echo of her scream. Rain was running down the living room windows and made it difficult to see, but Marianne was sure a man was sitting in the front seat of the truck. He was looking at the house. Is he looking at me? Did he hear me scream?

Adrenaline amplified her heartbeat in her ears. She did not notice another pounding from the far reaches of the strange house. She had no idea where David was – and only a small part of her brain even wondered why David hadn't come running at her scream.

But her instinct took over. She immediately tested the lock on the front door. Secure. The bolt thrown. She dashed into the kitchen. Windows closed. Locks snapped in place. She thought about a backdoor and saw that in the sunroom off the kitchen, there was a door that opened to the back deck. She quickly slipped into the room and checked the lock on that door. Secure. The bolt thrown. Standing there for just a moment in the darkened room of floor-to-ceiling framed windows, she felt terribly vulnerable. A bird in a cage. On display. Being watched.

Peering into the darkness, she could see nothing except the single glowing light at the end of the pier.

She slipped back into the kitchen, noting that the door between the sunroom and kitchen did not lock.

Marianne suddenly realized there was another sound filling her ears. Emily was screaming for her.

"Emily, I'm coming." She ran for the staircase, dismissing the rest of the house to the urgency of her daughter's safety. She thought, David can check... *where is he?*

"Mommy, mommy, mommy..." Upon seeing Marianne at the top of the stairs, Emily changed her chanted hysteria to "I'm scared, I'm scared, I'm scared..."

Marianne's first thought was to calm her daughter with her oft-used cooing voice, "It's okay, Emmie, Mommy's here." But when Emily asked with a nearly accusatory tone, "Why did you scream, Mommy?" Marianne's instinct to protect kicked in again.

In a decisive motion, she swept Emily into her arms, grabbing her daughter's beloved blanket and a lone plush rabbit.

"What is it, Mommy? Where are we going?"

Marianne said, "Let's find Daddy."

No longer hearing Emily crying gave David no comfort but only heightened his fear. And his imagination. He stood death-still in the closet, his shoulder throbbing. But he wasn't as frozen as he thought. His chest heaved incessantly. He was panting from exhaustion and tension. He stared at his hand gripping the locked doorknob.

What had happened? What *was* happening? Did Marianne scream because she was hurt? David's mind raced. Had she fallen? Had she burned herself?

No. Her scream had been a scream of fear.

But she screamed only once. Why was she no longer afraid?

Why wasn't she letting him out of the closet? He released the knob and looked around the edge of the door and the frame of the door jamb. Maybe *she* hadn't locked the door.

Maybe someone else did.

David remembered the pickup truck. And in his gut, he knew his once imagined threat had become real.

He smashed against the door again. He tried kicking at the doorknob but realized that would be futile. He turned looking for something in the closet to help him break open the door. There were plastic buckets and old rags and a dustpan and brush. On a high shelf he spotted a box of bullets for the .22. But no tools, nothing strong. Nothing useful.

The biggest thing in the closet was the four-foot long, wooden rifle case that contained Jim's .22, but of course the case was locked. David had no idea where the key was, but he knew it wouldn't be in the closet. Jim was too safety-conscious to keep the key near the locked case.

David picked it up. It was heavy and awkward, but he was determined to wield it. Holding the case like a battering ram, David smashed it into the doorknob. It made a loud, angry sound as the metal-edged, wooden case collided into the metal of the knob, the wood of the door and the sheet rock wall. The door held but plaster from the wall chipped and fell to the floor. David took aim again and began to pummel the knob repeatedly, like a pile driver. The pounding echoed in the closet accelerating David's adrenaline.

As Marianne crept along the corridor, past the kitchen, towards the master bedroom, she kept Emily quiet with a long soothing "ssshh," repeated with the rhythm of her soft steps. Emily was wide-eyed but knew that Mommy needed her to be quiet. Marianne whispered carefully, "David. David?"

A sudden BANG ahead of her stopped her in her tracks. It seemed to have come from where she assumed the master bedroom was. Then the banging became constant. Was someone trying to break into the house? The guy in the pickup truck must be outside trying to break in. Marianne hoped the locked doors would keep him at bay.

Cautiously she backpedaled toward the kitchen. Looking out the front window at the truck, Marianne could tell the front seat was empty now, despite the rain still pouring down. The glare of the outdoor lights was enough. It also confirmed that the truck, parked lengthwise between the brick pillars, would not allow the Mercedes to get past.

Looking around the driveway, she saw that either thick short hedges or two-foot ditches lined the property. There would be no escape by car. Besides, David probably had the keys with him.

Where *was* David? Panic started to take hold, but she could not risk shouting his name.

She thought for a moment. David would not have left the house. He must have heard her scream. The only reason he wouldn't have come running to her was... that he couldn't. Something must have happened to David. But how?

If someone – the trucker – was outside trying to break in, how could he have done something to David?

This wasn't adding up. She couldn't imagine what was happening. But the reality was this: a truck did follow them to SeaView, and that truck was now deliberately blocking her escape.

And she did need to escape. Because the banging down the hall was continuing and eventually that trucker would break in. Marianne needed to get out of the house. But where could she go?

As she turned, looking for a place to hide, a place to run to, a phone suddenly rang. Instinctively she thought it was a cellphone and felt for the pocket of her jeans. But her phone was upstairs in her bag.

The phone rang again. She didn't recognize the tone, but knew it was coming from the kitchen. It must be the house phone, she realized.

Emily whispered, "Phone, Mommy."

"I know, I know,' Marianne whispered back, hoisting her daughter higher up on her hip.

Marianne found the telephone on the kitchen counter.

"Hello? Hello?"

She heard a man's voice. "That must be Marianne. Hi, this is Jim. I was just checking to see if everything is okay."

Marianne almost burst at the sound of a friendly voice, "Oh Jim, thank God. No, it's not okay. Someone followed us, in a truck, and now they're blocking us from getting out."

"What? Who do you think followed you?"

"This guy in a pickup truck. And now he's trying to break into the house!"

"What? No one's trying to break into the house, Marianne."

"Yes, yes. The guy in the pickup truck who followed us."

"No, Marianne. I'm the guy in the pickup truck."

"What!!!"

"I thought for sure you'd go into the garage first."

Marianne was stunned. The attached garage. David didn't think there'd be room to park in there. But of course, that's another way into the house.

Jim said, "The garage is through the laundry room. Just off the kitchen."

Marianne turned and looked at the open door to the laundry room. She remembered seeing it earlier, but now there was a small amount of light, spilling under the door from what must be the garage. Marianne's mouth fell open. She started to shake as the coldest chill slid down her spine.

"Why don't you come into the garage now, Marianne? I've been waiting for you." Jim paused, then added, "And let's not tell David."

When the phone had rung a second time, David stopped pounding the doorknob with the rifle case. He needed to listen: what was going on? First Marianne had screamed. Then he thought he heard Emily crying. But once he started trying to smash his way out of the locked closet, he could only hear the rain attacking the house. Then the phone rang. The house phone. Twice. Did Marianne answer it? Or did it stop ringing on its own?

Or did someone else answer it?

David waited.

"Mommy?" Emily didn't like that Marianne had gotten quiet and was shaking.

Marianne looked at her daughter. The look on the child's face brought Marianne back. "It's okay, Emmie, Mommy knows what to do." Marianne adjusted Emily in the crook of her left arm and quietly went about opening drawer after drawer in the kitchen. On the fourth try, she found what she needed.

She tested the flashlight inside the drawer, and its powerful beam filled the space completely. The flashlight was long and heavy, Marianne knew it could become a weapon, too.

A door creaked. A quiet whisper, "Marianne?" It was not David.

"Mommy!" Emily was terrified.

"Quiet." Marianne's tone was sharp. She turned and in six quick strides, Marianne and Emily were through the kitchen door and into the sunroom. Marianne shone the flashlight into the backyard. The rain had stopped, and the full moon was shining brightly. The lawn fell away to the pier and the way seemed clear. Marianne unlocked the door, stepped out and quietly closed it behind her. Emily's weight dragged on her, so Marianne raised her higher in her arms. Emily dropped her blanket and plush rabbit.

"Mommy, bunny! Blankie!"

"They'll be safe, Emmie. Let's go!"

Jim looked out the kitchen window and saw Marianne running towards the pier with Emily bouncing on her hip. "Jesus!" He quickly flicked a light switch near the entrance to the sunroom and two strings of small white lights lit up the pier. He stepped out onto the back deck and bellowed, "Marianne, where do you think you're going?"

Startled at the sound of a man's voice – yelling *outside* the house – David smashed the rifle case at the doorknob again with a sudden burst of strength. The door frame finally splintered under the barrage. Stepping back into the bedroom, David noticed that the key to the door was lying on the floor. It had fallen out of the knob... or had he dropped it? Movement outside the window caught his attention. The pier was all lit up with Christmas lights. A tall man was walking towards the dock. Where was Marianne?

While David had been struggling to break through the closet door, he was trying to figure out one puzzle: the key to the rifle case. Now he had an idea. He went to the duck decoy that had held the key to the closet in its neck. Lifting the decoy, David found a hidden compartment door on the bottom and slid it open. A silver key fell to the carpet.

Marianne raced across the lawn, hunching slightly to lower her center of gravity – she didn't want to slip on the wet grass. She could feel the thick heavy blades below her feet, a hearty turfgrass that could tolerate the harsh salt-water from the inlet's tides. Her flats had become immediately soaked from the rain-drenched grass.

Emily bounced on her hip. "Where are we going, Mommy?"

"Boat ride."

"At nighttime? Why?"

"So we can see the moon and the stars, Emmie." But Emily spoke over her mother's words. "Where's Daddy?"

"I don't know. But I know he'll find us."

Suddenly the pier lit up with strands of small white lights strung along the pilings on either side of the wooden planks, stretching into the inlet. Marianne said, "Look. Like Christmas."

Once she reached the pier, Marianne turned towards the house for a quick look, but without moving the flashlight's beam from the planks in front of her. She could just make out the silhouette of a tall man coming through the sun-room's doors.

He yelled to her, "Marianne, where are you going?"

Marianne turned back to the pier and increased her speed. Despite the puddles she felt more comfortable running on the wood than on the grass. "Look, there's the boat." The cheery confidence in her voice was as much for herself as it was for Emily. She was certain she'd be able to drive the motorboat – she'd spent plenty of summer vacations driving her family's boat on Lake Hopatcong in New Jersey. But she also knew that there was a lot to do to ready a boat for launch.

The clouds had moved on, no longer blanketing the night sky. The full moon allowed Marianne to have a clear view of the boat.

It was tied to the dock at the bow and stern. A canvas tarp covered the outboard motor. Another tarp concealed the windshield, controls and seats.

As she ran splashing along the fifty feet of pier, she did a mental check list, considering the fastest way to get in the boat and away – which tasks were critical, which could be ignored.

Jim stepped onto the soaking wet grass in his boots. He called out, "WHY ARE YOU RUNNING? DON'T RUN FROM ME. THERE'S NO PLACE TO GO."

A shiver ran through Marianne, as she reached the end of the pier.

"Who's that man, Mommy?"

She put Emily down, and holding her hand, walked her down the ramp to the floating dock. "It's okay, Emmie, it's okay."

Marianne knew Jim was yelling at her, but she couldn't make out the words. As he got closer, his voice became louder and clearer. She looked up and saw he had just reached the far end of the pier. He was walking slowly.

"DON'T GO ON THE DOCK. YOU CAN GET HURT."

Marianne gently lifted Emily and placed her into the motorboat.

"YOU'RE PUTTING EMILY IN DANGER."

"Danger" was all Marianne could hear in her head.

"It's moving, Mommy."

"Just hold onto the side until I can climb in with you. I

have to make the boat ready."

Quickly Marianne unwound the bow rope from a cleat on the dock and tossed it onto the boat. As she moved towards the stern, she could hear Jim's boots pounding on the pier. He was running. "YOU'RE CRAZY IF YOU THINK I'M LETTING YOU GET ON THAT BOAT IN THE MIDDLE OF THE NIGHT."

The anger in his voice frightened her, and her trembling hands struggled with the next rope. Finally it was free of its cleat, and as Marianne stepped into the boat, she dropped the rope and reached for Emily.

But as she leaned forward, she was suddenly yanked backwards. Jim was already on the dock and in a powerful sweeping move, he had grabbed Marianne under her right arm and pulled her completely out of the boat. Jim yelled "NO," but his voice was drowned out by the screaming of both Marianne and Emily.

The motion of Marianne launching backwards from the boat actually pushed it away from the dock.

Marianne broke free from Jim's grip and dropped to the dock. Seeing Emily standing helpless in the boat crying hysterically, Marianne screamed, "Emily!"

BANG!

The sudden gunshot startled Marianne, and Jim cried out, crashing to the dock beside her. Blood splattered her clothing and the dock. Even in the limited glow from the Christmas lights and the moon, Marianne could see that Jim's ear had been blown away.

Turning she saw David standing in the middle of the dock with a rifle aimed from his shoulder. For a moment, their eyes met. Then David snapped to and shouted, "Emily!"

Marianne sprang to her feet, "Just hold on Emmie, hold on to the side and kneel down."

The boat was now some twenty feet away, the swift current pushing it along the inlet.

Marianne dove headfirst into the water. Emily screamed again too frightened to move, and when the boat rocked, she fell down crying. Marianne burst from the water with a loud grunt, exasperated by the cold water. "Emmie, I'm coming."

David dropped the rifle and ran to the dock. He could not see Emily, but he could hear her crying from inside the boat which was now thirty feet from the dock. He watched as Marianne cut through the water towards the boat. He knew she was a strong swimmer but realized she wouldn't be able to climb into the boat on her own. He remembered there was no ladder on the back of the boat. He'd have to follow her. David looked briefly at Jim, lying motionless on the dock. The blood on his face, the blood on the wooden planks, was too much and David looked away. Think.

He patted his pockets, then removed his wallet and car keys and dropped them onto the dock. He ripped off his soaking wet socks. He shouted, "Marianne, grab the boat. I'm coming to help. Emily, just lie down, baby, Mommy and Daddy... you'll be okay." He could still hear her crying.

At the edge of the dock, David looked up and down the length of the dark inlet. The memory of the day he saw the dorsal fin of the sandbar shark flashed in his mind. "Fuck it." David jumped in the water and began swimming towards the boat. He could see that Marianne had already reached it.

When David caught up to the drifting boat, Emily was no longer crying. Marianne was talking to her, all sing-song, telling her to look at the beautiful full moon and all the millions and millions of stars.

"Marianne, are you okay?"

"Yes. We just have to get out of here."

"Put your foot in my hands and I'll push you up onto the boat. Then you can pull me in."

With no more words, Marianne grabbed high on the side of the boat, and David hoisted her upwards. The motion pushed him below the water, but a swift kick of his legs and Marianne rose just enough to push her body into the boat. She grabbed Emily and squeezed her with a loving hug. She kissed her head as Emily squirmed, "Mommy you're all wet and cold. Let go of me."

Marianne leaned over the side of the boat, and she and David locked arms. She pulled backwards with all her might as David slid his right leg up the side. Grabbing the top, he pulled himself over and into the boat as Marianne crashed backwards next to Emily.

David slid over to his wife and daughter. "Emmie, are you okay?"

"Don't hug me Daddy, you're wet, too."

"I know, baby. I went for a swim. Mommy, too. It's fun."

Marianne burst out crying and hugged David. "Why, David, why?"

His face pressed close to her ear, he whispered, "I don't know, honey, I don't know. But I shot him. I shot him. We have to go back and get to the police."

"Why's Mommy crying, Daddy?"

"It's okay, Emily. Mommy's not sad. Mommy's happy because we're all okay. We're all safe."

"Safe from that man?"

David blurted out, "Yes, Emmie, safe from that man."

"That man was a monster?"

Marianne spoke, calmly, "No, Emmie, there are no monsters."

They were all jostled when the port side of the boat bumped into the far side of the inlet, where the reeds stood three feet above the boat.

"We have to start the motor. Do you think you could do that?" David asked his wife.

"I'm sure I can, if there's gasoline. I'll deal with that. Look for life jackets. Do you think the inlet would lead us to the ocean?"

"Marianne, we're not going in the ocean at night. That's insane. Let's just go back to the dock. We'll get in our car and go find the police."

"I don't want to go back there."

David grabbed her firmly and whispered in her ear.

She looked at him, "Are you sure?" He nodded slowly. "I don't want Emily to see."

David answered, "She won't. I'll take care of that."

Marianne moved to the stern and removed the tarp covering the outboard motor. She had to slide her cold wet fingers under each snap to pull them open, making a series of loud popping sounds.

"Bang, bang," said Emily. "Like when Daddy shot the man."

David's head snapped back to look at Marianne who stared back, mouth agape.

David said quietly, "Come over here, Emily. Help Daddy make the boat ready. Mommy's going to drive us." David folded back the tarp that covered the steering wheel and controls. He plopped Emily into the captain's seat.

"Mar'e, there's a key in the ignition."

"Thank God." When she was done with the tarp, she reached over to the side of the motor and pushed in the primer ball, which released oil to prime the engine. "If it's got gas, we should be all set." Marianne stepped to the console. "David, sit there with Emily." She pointed to a cushioned seat on the port side. Standing in front of the steering wheel, Marianne turned the key in the ignition and the engine started up immediately.

Emily jumped a little, but yelled, "Yeah."

Marianne clicked on the running lights. "Let's go home." She spun the wheel and threw the gearshift into forward. She expertly turned the boat in a tight turn and quickly drove the boat back the now fifty feet to the dock.

As the boat neared the dock, David said to Emily, "I'm giving you an important job, Emily. You hold onto this side of the boat. It's called starboard. And your job is to count the stars. You stay there and count out loud until I call you. Okay?"

"Okay, Daddy. I see a lot of stars."

"Good. Now count them."

"I see one. I see two. …"

To keep her daughter from seeing the carnage on the dock, Marianne pulled in on the port-side. She cut the engine as the boat slipped alongside the dock. David moved to the bow, grabbed the rope tied to the forward cleat and was set to jump up on the dock. But seeing the dock he quickly turned to look at Marianne. She too was looking at the dock.

There was a gory puddle of blood. But no Jim.

They made eye contact. David motioned for her to quiet Emily. Marianne whispered and hugged Emily as David jumped to the dock, used the rope to steady the boat, then secured the rope to a cleat on the dock. He scanned the pier. No sign of Jim. At the edge of the dock, he retrieved his wallet and keys, but left his socks. Inching up the ramp to the pier he looked down its length. No Jim. There was something lying on the planks, though, about halfway. David hoped it was the rifle

He motioned to Marianne to follow him.

Marianne swung Emily onto the dock, holding her attention so that she wouldn't see the splattered blood. They moved up behind David.

David whispered, "Let's pretend we're quiet little mice, sneaking up on the house."

"I'm scared."

"Emily, there's nothing to be scared of." Marianne held David's stare for a moment.

They moved along the pier slowly, David leading Emily by the hand, crouching, Marianne following, also crouching, ready to run, in either direction.

As they approached the rifle lying in the middle of the planks, Emily asked, "What's that, Daddy?"

"It's nothing. Just leave it."

Marianne said, "No, David, take it."

As David turned to argue, he stood tall, "Listen."

"What is it?"

"Listen." Marianne also stood up. Listening, she was suddenly aware of all the sounds of the night. The crickets and other nighttime insects that chirped across the inlet. The lapping sounds as the current pushed and pulled against the marsh reeds. She could also hear the boat bumping against the pilings.

"What?"

"Truck."

Marianne listened again. Of course, she thought, that hum. Clearly an engine, but deeper like a truck's. And definitely pulling further away.

The words rushed out of Marianne, "Now's our chance, we won't be blocked in. Go, go!"

David didn't understand, but he scooped up Emily and followed Marianne who dashed ahead along the pier, across the grass and towards the house.

Through the sunroom and into the kitchen they ran. Marianne looked out the front window. The driveway was still lit by the outdoor lights. There was no truck blocking their escape.

"Go to the car, David, I'll grab my bag from upstairs."

"NO. We'll come back with the police. We have to go now."

"Right."

Marianne led the way out of the house as David slipped his wet bare feet into his shoes at the front door. He carried Emily down the front steps and across the driveway to their car.

At the Mercedes, Marianne took Emily from David, "I'll get her in."

Without warning, the heavens opened up again and fresh rain pummeled the car.

David ran around the car, slid behind the wheel, and revved the engine. "Let's go."

"She's not buckled."

"Now!"

Marianne closed Emily's door, jumped into the front seat, "Okay, go." David backed out of the driveway, squealing the wheels on the wet pavement. As soon as the car straightened out and was headed along the road back to the entrance to SeaView, Marianne spun around in her seat and reached into the back to try to finish buckling Emily into her car seat.

"Are you scared, Mommy?"

"No, baby, there's nothing to be scared of."

"You're shaking."

"I'm just a little cold because my clothes are wet."

"Is Daddy shaking?" Emily fidgeted to try to see her father.

The dashboard on the Mercedes began to ping. Instinctively, David muttered, "Seat belt, Mar'e." He was concentrating on the rain on the windshield, the slick road, the speedometer now touching 60.

"Stay still, Emily, so Mommy can buckle you. Safety first, right?"

David leaned slightly forward trying to see up ahead. There was something just beyond the range of the Mercedes' headlights. Then it was quickly in view.

The truck. Not far from the closed iron gate.

It was half off the road, a front tire down in the three-foot ditch that framed every road in the SeaView development. Standing in the middle of the road, clearly unsteady, was Jim. He had his back to the speeding Mercedes. The way he moved, the way he was bent over, David could tell Jim was in agony. He was pressing something, maybe a towel, against the left side of his head where David had shot him.

Jim turned towards the car.

David thought quickly. He wanted to drive around Jim, but he'd have to slow down and wait for the gate's sensors to automatically open.

David warned Marianne, "It's Jim."

Marianne spun in her seat, "Where?!"

"He crashed off the road."

"Don't slow down!"

They watched as Jim steadied himself in the middle of the road. He raised his right hand and pointed at them. There was something in his hand.

"He's got a gun!"

Emily screamed at the fear in her mother's voice. "Monster!"

David shouted, "Nooooo!" as he floored the accelerator aiming right for Jim.

The impact sent Jim smashing into the windshield. Blinded, shocked, David didn't have time to stop. The Mercedes crashed full speed into the closed iron gate.

A light rain fell, barely visible in the headlight beams of the four patrol cars and the two ambulances that lined the pitched road leading into SeaView.

The policeman walked over to the volunteer EMT team. "Better bag all three bodies."

"You done with him, too?" the head technician asked.

"Gimme a minute with him."

"He's in shock."

"Suppose so."

The policeman, a barrel-chested veteran with a bushy

gray moustache, pulled himself into the ambulance and sat across from David. "Mr. Jackson?"

Sitting upright on a gurney, David was bundled in a blanket. His forehead was bandaged, an IV tube leading to his arm. He stared out the back of the ambulance, at the gate.

"Mr. Jackson, I'm Sheriff Lawrence. They're gonna take you to the hospital now. I'll see you there later. Before you go, is there a statement you'd like to make? Can you tell us what happened?"

David spoke. "He had a gun. He pointed it at us. He was going to shoot. He had a gun."

At that moment, another policeman came to the back of the ambulance. The sheriff asked him, "Paul, any luck finding a gun?"

"Not yet, sir. All we found is this." The policeman, a young man in his 20s, held up a black plastic device.

The sheriff asked him, "That to open the gate?"

The officer, Paul Shelley, responded, "No sir, that's what I thought, too. But it didn't work. Not on that gate anyway. I think it looks more like a garage door opener."

The sheriff let out a sigh. "Why would a guy, shot in the head, be waving a garage door opener in the middle of the road?"

Officer Shelley knew better than to answer one of Sheriff Lawrence's rhetorical questions. David looked at Shelley, then turned to look at Lawrence. His eyes filled with tears, "Why?"

Officer Shelley drove between the brick pillars that stood as sentinels leading to the property at the end of the road, where a large yellow house looked out onto the inlet. He stopped his squad car in front of the attached garage. The rotating lights atop the car's roof chased their red beams along the front of the house and into the darkness beyond.

Shelley pointed the black plastic device at the garage and pressed the button. The garage door sprung to action and began to climb. "Knew it," the police officer said to no one.

An interior light automatically came on in the garage. As the door climbed, Shelley could see that the floor was especially clean. Tool chests and other equipment were all well-organized and tidy. There were no cars inside but plenty of space to fit two – except… "What the hell?" Shelley said out loud.

When the door was fully open, the motor clanked and shut off. Shelley stared inside.

The beams from the squad car's headlights flooded the garage, and the red lights raced now along the inside walls as well.

Shelley exited his car and entered the garage

There were countless streamers hanging from the ceiling. Helium balloons, all red, white or blue, dozens of them, bumped along the ceiling.

On the back wall, a homemade sign was hung. The letters read, "Happy Birthday David."

KEVIN JOHN WINDORF

Born and raised in New York City, Kevin John Windorf attended New York University and Fordham College, where he studied creative writing, poetry, and film production. While pursuing a career in communications, he has written extensively in a wide range of creative formats including screenplays, short fiction, and poetry.

He is the author of the short story collection "The Serpent Bearer: 13 Stories of Suspense" (Quindorian Press 2018), the novella "The Gate" (Quindorian Press, 2014), and the story cycle "Speaking In Tongues" (Quindorian Press, 2013).

In 2013, his short story "Call From The Cabin" was featured on NPR's "All Things Considered" as a program favorite from its Three Minute Fiction contest.

www.kevinwindorf.com.

www.ingramcontent.com/pod-product-compliance
Lightning Source LLC
Chambersburg PA
CBHW070809120626
46557CB00002B/782